# Green Green

## A Community Gardening Story

By Marie Lamba and Baldev Lamba

Pictures by Sonia Sánchez

Farrar Straus Giroux
New York

Green green,
fresh and clean.

Brown brown,
dig the ground.

Rakes scrape.
Seeds in rows.
Tamp and water.
The garden grows.

Brown brown,
dig the ground.

Dozers lift.
Concrete flows.

Stone and metal,
the city grows . . .

and GROWS.

Green green,
in between.

Squirrel gray,
pigeon blue,
weeds and wildflowers,
litter, too.

Brown brown,
dig the ground?

Brown brown,
dig the ground!

Lift and clear.
Shovel rows.
Working together,
our garden grows . . .

and GROWS . . .

AND
GROWS.

Green green,
keep it clean.

# Make Your World More Green Green

A city is an exciting place to live, but there are a lot of buildings and pavement covering the ground. Where can you dig and make things grow?

At a community garden!

These gardens are formed when neighbors get together to create their own bit of **GREEN GREEN**, often on an empty lot. Folks work hard to clear trash from the site, and then it's **BROWN BROWN, DIG THE GROUND** time. They grow flowers to enjoy, and healthy fresh herbs, vegetables, and fruits to eat. These beautiful, useful gardens also become homes for bees, butterflies, and birds.

You can make your own world more **GREEN GREEN**, no matter where you live.

Is there a community garden nearby? Then join in the fun. If not, maybe you can help your neighbors start one.

You can also create your own garden at home. Don't have ground to dig? Then you can use planters made out of recycled items like plastic bottles and food containers. Decorate the containers, plant your seeds, and set your new planters in a sunny spot, watering as needed. Now watch your garden grow and **Grow** and **GROW**!

To learn more about community gardens and discover other ways you can be **GREEN GREEN**, visit marielamba.com/books-etc/green-green.

# Bees and Butterflies Need Your Help!

Our world relies on bees, butterflies, and other pollinators to keep it GREEN GREEN. Pollinators are insects that visit flowers and spread pollen from plant to plant. Without them, most of the world's flowering plants wouldn't be able to grow fruits or the seeds needed to produce future plants!

Honeybees and monarch butterflies are great pollinators, but they are in danger of disappearing. Too little green space and too many pesticides mean there are fewer and fewer of them fluttering and buzzing about. Here's how you can help:

1. **Become a Honeybee Hero!** Say NO to weed-killing chemicals. Instead, "bee safe" and pull weeds in your garden by hand, or spray weeds with a mix of white vinegar and a few tablespoons of liquid dish detergent.

2. **Be a Monarch Butterfly Buddy!** Monarch butterflies MUST have milkweed plants to survive. They lay eggs on them, and their caterpillars eat only milkweed. Help by planting milkweed in your yard, or getting your school to grow it.

3. **Be GREEN GREEN!** Grow lots of plants with flowers that pollinators can visit.

## BEE and BUTTERFLY Decorations

Welcome bees and butterflies to your own special bit of GREEN GREEN with this craft reusing everyday items.

**You need:**

- clothespin
- waterproof markers or paint
- pipe cleaner
- plastic shopping bag
- scissors

**Directions:**

1. Cut bag into a 6"x 6" square for the wings.
   Decorate both sides with colorful designs!
2. Draw eyes and a smile on the clothespin.
3. Clamp the decorated square with the clothespin to create wings.
4. Curl the tips of the pipe cleaner into antennae, then clamp them with the clothespin above the wings. For a bee, draw stripes on the clothespin body.

In memory of our dear brother Stephen Busterna,
who so loved to garden and to help his community
—M.L. & B.L.

For my family—for all the time we spent working
in our little 'country house'

—S.S.

Farrar Straus Giroux Books for Young Readers
An imprint of Macmillan Publishing Group, LLC
175 Fifth Avenue, New York 10010

Text copyright © 2017 by Marie Lamba and Baldev Lamba
Pictures copyright © 2017 by Sonia Sánchez
All rights reserved
Color separations by Embassy Graphics
Printed in China by RR Donnelley Asia Printing Solutions Ltd.,
Dongguan City, Guangdong Province
Designed by Roberta Pressel
First edition, 2017
10  9  8  7  6  5  4  3  2  1

mackids.com

Library of Congress Cataloging-in-Publication Data
Names: Lamba, Marie, author. | Lamba, Baldev, author. | Sánchez, Sonia,
    1983– illustrator.
Title: Green green : a community gardening story / by Marie and Baldev
    Lamba ; pictures by Sonia Sánchez.
Description: First edition. | New York : Farrar Straus Giroux, 2017. |
    Summary: In the city an abandoned lot squeezed between two buildings
    becomes a community garden.
Identifiers: LCCN 2016034913 | ISBN 9780374327972 (hardcover)
Subjects: | CYAC: Stories in rhyme. | Community gardens—Fiction. |
    Gardens—Fiction. | City and town life—Fiction.
Classification: LCC PZ8.3.L2713 Gr 2017 | DDC [E]—dc23
LC record available at https://lccn.loc.gov/2016034913

Our books may be purchased in bulk for promotional, educational, or
business use. Please contact your local bookseller or the Macmillan Corporate
and Premium Sales Department at (800) 221-7945 ext. 5442 or by e-mail at
MacmillanSpecialMarkets@macmillan.com.